A Bear Called Sunday

A Bear
Called Sunday

by Axel Hacke

Illustrations by Michael Sowa

Translated from the German by Rosemary Davidson

BLOOMSBURY

First published by Verlag Antje Kunstmann GmbH,
Munchen 2001 under the title *Ein Bär Namens Sontag* by Axel Hacke,
with illustrations by Michael Sowa

First published in Great Britain 2003

This translation copyright © 2003 by Rosemary Davidson

© Verlag Antje Kunstmann, Munich, 2001

The moral right of the author has been asserted

A CIP catalogue record for this book is available from the British Library

ISBN 0 7475 6655 0

10 9 8 7 6 5 4 3 2 1

Typeset by Richard Horne

Printed and bound by Tien Wah Press, Singapore

For David

When I was a small boy, I had a silent little bear called Sunday.

One morning when I woke up the bear was lying beside me, looking very new.

'What's your name?' I asked him. But the bear didn't answer. He just stared straight ahead.

'What's your name, bear?' I asked again. But the bear didn't bat an eyelid. He didn't answer at all.

If he won't tell me his name, I thought to myself, well… Maybe it's simply that he *can't* tell me, I thought. Maybe he can't tell me because he *has* no name. If that is the case, I thought, then *I* must give him a name. Every bear has to have a name. Otherwise how can you call them when you need them?

I looked at the bear for a long time and thought about what I should call him. Finally, I decided to call him Bear-that-was-lying-beside-me-in-bed-one-morning. I thought about this name for a while. Then it occurred to me that Bear-that-was-lying-beside-me-in-bed-one-morning was a very long name for such a little bear. He really was only a very little bear, just as I was only a little boy at the time. To be honest, he wasn't even as long as my right arm.

So I called the bear Sunday, because it was on a Sunday morning that I found him lying in bed beside me for the first time, and so why not call him Sunday?

And that is how this story began.

From that morning on, the bear called Sunday and I were never apart. When I went on the swings at the playground, Sunday sat

on the swing next to me. When I went for a ride on my bicycle, Sunday came along too, wedged on to the luggage rack. And when I went to the toilet, Sunday sat next to me on a little potty.

We were the best of friends. And of course Sunday came to bed with me every night. I couldn't close my eyes unless he was beside me. I would put my arm around the little bear and stroke his bear fur, to feel for sure that he was beside me. Then I would bury my nose in his soft bear coat to smell that he was beside me. Then I would put my ear to his bear tummy to hear that he was beside me. Only when I had done all these things, and when I was quite sure that Sunday really was there beside me, I'd fall asleep and Sunday, well he'd have been sleeping for a long time already, snoring little bear snores – bear-sch… bear-sch…

But one morning, when I woke up, I looked at the little bear lying there beside me and thought: does Sunday love me as much as I love him? He never says anything. He never gives me a hug. He never gives me a kiss. He just sits there. Or lies. Or stands. And looks straight ahead. But he doesn't *do* anything, he never *does* anything at all. And if he never *does* anything, maybe he's not *really* alive. And if he's not *really* alive, how can he love me?

I lifted my little bear up in the air and shook him. Next I stood up, laid him on the floor and jumped on his tummy with both feet. Then I took a little toy hammer and hit him on his head as hard as I could.

But Sunday just lay there and stared straight ahead.

'I don't believe it!' I thought. 'It's just not possible that a bear lets himself be treated like that.'

I put him under my arm and went to have breakfast. There was a glass of milk and a plate of bread and honey on the table, as there was every morning. I told my mother that Sunday wanted milk and bread with honey as well that morning. So my mother poured some milk into a glass and made some bread and honey and put them in front of Sunday.

But he didn't eat a thing. And he didn't drink. He only stared straight ahead.

I took the glass and tried to give him some milk, but it just ran down his snout, because he hadn't opened it, and when I tried to feed him the bread and honey all I managed to do was to get his mouth and fur all sticky – because he wouldn't eat a thing.

'Sunday's stupid!' I shouted. 'I don't love him at all!' And I took the bear and flung him right across the table against the wall.

My mother lifted the bear up. 'What are you doing to poor Sunday?!' she cried. Then she said he smelt of milk and his fur was all sticky. She put him into the washing-machine and washed him. Then I thought – you can't do that – you can't put a little bear in the washing-machine – how will he breathe? But the drum of the washing-machine was already going round, so I sat in front of it and looked through the round window as Sunday got washed. Even then he just stared straight ahead. But as I watched it suddenly seemed to me that his eyes looked very, very, very sad.

When my mother took him out of the washing-machine again, Sunday was soaking wet. All day long he had to hang on the clothes-horse to dry with clothes-pegs stuck on his ears. Every

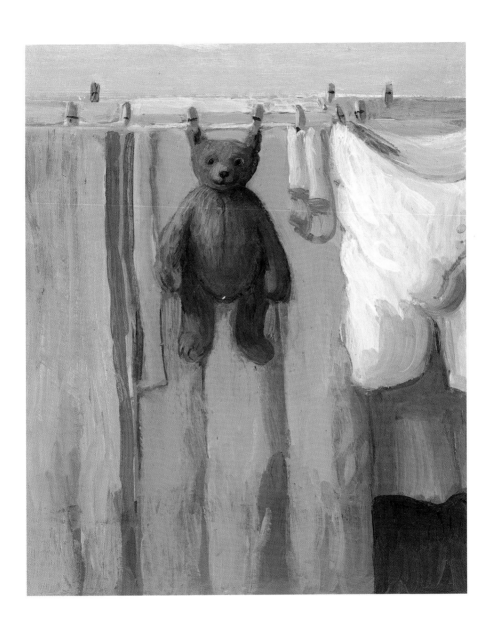

time I went past him I thought he looked at me with a very, very, very sad expression. And once when I walked past him particularly slowly, I thought I heard him whisper to me: 'I never thought you would leave me hanging here like this. I thought we were friends and now here I am dangling from this clothes-horse like a pair of underpants.'

That evening was the first since I had got him that Sunday didn't sleep in my bed with me. My mother said he was still too wet. So I had to go to sleep on my own – for the first night in a very long time I had to go to sleep all alone. But I couldn't – I just tossed and turned...

... and then, from the hall where the clothes-horse was, I thought I heard the bear softly sing:

'I'm just a little wa-hash-bear,
Hanging here on the line
As if I a piece of washing were
Can no one hear I'm crying?'

I lay in bed and thought about what a wa-hash-bear might be, and what Sunday meant when he sang that he was a wa-hash-bear, and then I thought how much I wanted to stroke his fur and bury my nose in his soft bear coat and put my ear to his little bear tummy – but I couldn't...

Oh! I can tell you this: that was one of the saddest nights of my whole life.

When I finally did fall asleep, I had a dream – well, actually I had two dreams – one very short one and one very long one.

First I dreamed that I was grown up and didn't have a teddy bear to cuddle any more. I was lying in my bed with a suit on, and a shirt and a tie. My father lay in my right arm. He was very small, much smaller than me and he was drinking milk from a giant baby's bottle. In my left arm, lay my mother. She was also tiny and was eating a huge slice of bread and honey. Suddenly my father dropped his bottle on to the floor because it was empty, and my mother had finished her bread and honey. Both shouted at once: 'Read us something!'

I had the fright of my life. 'But I can't read,' I said.

'Read us something anyway!' they shouted. And before I could have an even bigger fright than the one I'd just had, the short dream ended. The long dream started immediately after that.

In this dream I lived in a toyshop. The toyshop belonged to an old bear called Mr Teddy Bear, who always wore a blue overall. A parrot sat on his shoulder. Mr Teddy Bear stood behind a long wooden counter. From time to time, the door swung open and other bears came into the shop, men bears in grey suits, lady bears in pretty dresses and bear children who swarmed about impatiently in front of the counter, barely able to wait for Mr Teddy Bear to show them the toys he had for sale.

Each time a man or lady bear or a bear child came into the shop, the parrot on the shop owner's shoulder would cry: 'T-o-y-s! V-e-r-y l-o-v-e-l-y t-o-y-s! W-o-n-d-e-r-f-u-l t-o-y-s!'

Behind the counter there was a huge cabinet containing lots of boxes, big ones and little ones. Inside these boxes were the toys.

Each time Mr Teddy Bear wanted to get a box down from the cabinet to show someone its contents, he had to climb up a long ladder with the parrot on his shoulder, and as he climbed the shelves would make a creaking noise. It was a very old toyshop.

Yes, that's right, you've understood. I *lived* in this toyshop. I lived there with lots of other children in a big box quite high up in the cabinet. And every now and again the old toyshop owner climbed high up on his ladder to fetch our box down and show us to his customers. Then we'd be taken out and demonstrated.

There were father bears who wanted a little boy for their bear sons to play with. There were granny bears looking for a little girl for their granddaughter to cuddle. And there were little bears who wanted to buy a little boy or girl for themselves and who counted the pocket money in their hand over and over again to see if they had enough.

Sometimes one of us would be sold and we'd wave goodbye furtively to whoever it was as they left the shop.

Once, an old aunt bear came in, smelling of perfume. She lifted me up and squeezed me so tightly that I could hardly breathe.

'Oh no!' I thought, gasping for air. 'I hope she doesn't take me home!'

Another time, an uncle polar bear came in, you know the kind with white fur? He smelt of schnapps and threw me high up into the air. But he didn't catch me and I found myself sprawled on the ground, my head buzzing. Some bears are just so stupid!

'Oh no!' I thought, 'I don't want to belong to a stupid drunk uncle bear!'

And once a couple came in with their fat little son who they called 'Windipops'. Windipops was eating jelly babies out of a bag, one after the other. He took me in his fat little arms and gave me a great big slobbery lick – slobber, slobber, slobber.

'Oh no!' I thought, 'I don't want to be licked to death by this fat little Windipops!'

I was in luck. None of them bought me, and so at the end of the day Mr Teddy Bear would put me back on the shelf in the box.

I was glad about this because it was nice living in the toyshop. In the evening when the old bear had closed up for the night and had gone into his flat at the back of the shop with his parrot, we children would push the lids off our boxes and climb out. Then we'd choose toys for ourselves from the other boxes and play with whatever we liked.

We drove about in toy cars. We cooked ourselves some dinner on a dolls' house oven. We rode toy elephants. And so on. Sometimes we didn't have time to tidy everything away again before Mr Teddy Bear came back into the shop in the morning.

We never let him see us though. We never let him find out that we played secretly. Sometimes we had to scurry back to our boxes as soon as we heard him coming, leaving toys lying on the floor or on the counter.

When that happened Mr Teddy Bear would grumble, shake his big head and tidy everything away, while the parrot on his shoulder shrieked: 'Mucky bears! Tidy up! Tidy up! Tidy bears! Bunch of layabouts!'

'Shut up!' Mr Teddy Bear would growl, suddenly baring his teeth like a dangerous wild bear.

The parrot would squawk and flap up to the very highest shelf. If all was quiet again we'd go to sleep in our boxes until the first customers came in.

But one day I was sold too. A father bear came into the shop and had all the children shown to him. As soon as he saw me he smiled, lifted me up and said, 'I like this one. I'll take him.'

'He costs £30,' said Mr Teddy Bear. I never would have imagined that I cost £30 – so-o-o much money. But there I was, stuck head first into a bag, my legs poking out of the top. The father bear took the bag and left the shop.

Outside in the street I wriggled myself carefully the right way up – slowly, slowly, so that the bear didn't notice, until my head

poked out of the top instead of my feet.

Remember, until then I'd only ever lived in the toyshop and had never even been outside. I saw the Land of the Bears for the first time and I have to say, it was amazing. There were bears everywhere, bears in hats, bears in coats, bears with briefcases, bears on bicycles, bears on skateboards, bear sweethearts, bears on a clanging tram...

We walked through the streets. A bear was walking a little tiger on a leash. The tiger sniffed at me and frightened the wits out of me. I almost cried out but the bear who had bought me scared it off with a wave of his paw.

Then we came to a taxi rank – but the taxis in this Land of the Bears weren't cars at all but carriages drawn by four pigs. We got into one. On the coach-box sat a bear in a leather coat and cap. He shouted, 'Ha!' and the pigs grunted and pulled the carriage away. We drove through a large park with a lake. By the side of the lake a polar bear was standing beside a sign which read 'Ice floes for hire'. Other polar bears were pressing money into his paw and

going for a row on the lake on an ice floe. And some of them had great big lollies in the shape of penguins. They licked and sucked at them with their red tongues and laughed.

An apartment block stood at the edge of the park and that was where the bear that had bought me lived. He got out of the pig-taxi. On the ground floor of the building there was a bamboo shop in which a panda bear stood shouting, 'Bamboo shoots! Finest bamboo shoots!' Next door there was a fish shop where a big grizzly bear in a white apron was scooping a big fish out of a tank with his paw.

The bear lived on the third floor and as we entered the flat his wife came to greet him. The bear took me out of the shopping bag. 'Oh, he's so sweet!' the lady bear cried. She kissed me with her bear mouth and smelled of honey – ohhhh! She smelt so wonderfully of honey. I wished she would never stop kissing me, so wonderful was her honey smell.
The lady bear took me and wrapped me in wrapping paper – it was soft and it tickled my nose. When I was all wrapped up I had to sneeze and nearly burst out of the paper. Then I fell asleep.

When I woke up I could hear the man bear and the lady bear singing – they were singing 'Happy Bearthday to You, Happy Bearthday dear Sunday, Happy Bearthday to you.' I felt myself suddenly being lifted up in my wrapping paper. Someone ripped the paper off and suddenly I saw a little bear who looked very familiar. But just then I couldn't think why.

The little bear looked at me and cried: 'Oh, but he's lovely.' Then he hugged me – he pressed his soft furry face to mine – he touched my nose with his cool bear-nose – more important than anything it seemed he loved me very much. He picked me up and danced around the room with me.

'What are you going to call your little boy then, Sunday?' asked the mother bear. The little bear answered excitedly, 'I'll call him, ummm, ummm... I'll call him Axel.'

Then I was very happy because I really am called Axel, you see, and because the little bear had by chance given me exactly the right name.

We spent the whole day together – whatever the little bear called Sunday was doing, I was there too. I had some of his birthday cake. When he played in the sandpit I sat next to him. I sat wedged into the luggage rack when Sunday went for a spin on his bicycle. And when he went to the toilet I sat next to him on a little potty.

When the little bear went to bed at night, I had to lie beside him. Sunday would close his eyes and put his arms around me and stroke me to feel that I was there. Then he would snuffle with his nose against my skin to smell that I was there. Then he would hold his ear to my tummy to hear that I was there. And when he had done all those things and was quite sure that I really was lying there beside him, Sunday would fall asleep.
And then?

And then, well, the dream ended and I woke up. When I woke I saw that the little bear was lying beside me as he had every night and every morning, although he had still been hanging on the clothes-horse the evening before. Somehow during the night he had come into my bed. He smelt all freshly washed and was still a

tiny bit damp.

But I didn't mind at all.